SEA

Crystal
Kingdom

Iliana

The
Forest

Alhambra

Volcano of the
Princess
of the Night

Mount
Nereid

Kingdom
of the Frogs

Lake Garia

Prison of
the Blizzard
Wizard

RAMION

The Land
of Lost Hair

FRANKIE AND THE DANCING FURIES

Published by

Perronet Press

www.ramion-books.com

Copyright © Text and illustrations

Frank Hinks 2018

A CIP record for this book is available from the British Library

ISBN: 9781909938090

Printed in China by CP Printing Ltd.
Layout by Jennifer Stephens

TALES of RAMION

FRANKIE AND THE DANCING FURIES

FRANK HINKS

Perronet

2018

TALES of RAMION

THE GARDENER

Lord of Ramion, guardian and protector

SNUGGLE

Dream Lord sent to protect the boys from the witch Griselda

JULIUS ALEXANDER BENJAMIN

Three brothers who long for adventure

SCROOEY-LOOEY

Greedy, rude, half-mad rabbit, a friend of the boys

SUSAN

The boys' mother as a child

THE BOYS' FATHER

Loves rock and roll, very keen on dancing

MAKI AND FEY

Elven children

GRISELDA THE GRUNCH

A witch who longs to eat the boys

THE DIM DAFT DWARVES

Julioso, Aliano, Benjio, Griselda's guards

BORIS

Griselda's pet skull, strangely fond of her

THE DANCING FURIES

Allecto, Megaera, Tisiphone formerly Goddesses of Vengeance

PRINCESS OF
THE NIGHT

*Lord of Nothingness,
source of evil*

ALBEE
THE ALBATROSS

*Spy of the Princess,
harbinger of doom*

GNARGS

Warrior servants of the Princess

CHAPTER ONE

Before mankind walked the earth, the Princess of the Night, a mixture of stinking gases, oozed from place to place, leaving behind the stench of evil. With the coming of mankind she took on a mockery of human form, the gases solidifying just enough to bear clothes and carry a magic staff, but at night her body returned to its malign essence. The gases gathered in an urn of adamantine stone, which light, love, joy, laughter and dreams (all the things the Princess hated most) could not penetrate. For long centuries the urn stood upon the ground in her lair, a live volcano not far from the Garden in the Land of Ramion, until one day, when looking for new specimens for her living sculpture collection, she came upon two boys playing soldiers, standing to attention. Turning the boys to stone, she got her servants to place a stone shelf across their heads and put the urn upon the shelf, a suitable resting place (or so the Princess thought).

This day started like any other. The Princess awoke. With a hiss she rose from the urn. But as she assumed her mockery of human form she felt a sense of excitement. Strange. It was not like her to feel emotion. She wondered why. Then she remembered. She had bought the body of Boris the Skull from Charlie Stench the Body Collector. She had ordered her servants to place it in the anteroom beyond the Sculpture Hall. Picking up her magic staff she hurried through the Sculpture Hall, taking no notice of her collection of children frozen in the act of playing. She entered the anteroom. Slowly she contemplated the body of Boris.

The Princess should have been happy. It was the first adult body in her collection. As bodies go it was not bad. It had arms, legs, fingers and thumbs, but something was wrong. The Princess was not satisfied. She cried out to her servants, "Something is missing! I am not sure what, but something is not right!"

Her servants shuffled their feet, looked anxiously at their fingernails and coughed nervously, not daring to tell the Princess what was missing, until one braver (or more stupid) than the rest said, "It doesn't have a head!"

"The head! Are you suggesting I did not realise it does not have a head?"

"No, no, no, no!"

"Are you saying I am a moron?"

"No, no, no, no!"

The Princess raised her magic staff and, with a deep groan, the servant vanished in a puff of stinking gas. The other servants fell to their knees, kissing the hem of her dress, begging for mercy. The Princess ignored them. Speaking to herself she hissed, "I must get the head. But how? I shall use that stupid witch Griselda. She will not realise she is following my commands."

When Griselda awoke next morning an idea was whirling round her head: she had no idea where it had come from. "I must summon the elements," she muttered to herself. "I must make the boys travel to me. Roast Julius! Stewed Alexander! Benjamin on toast! Just what I always wanted."

Hardly knowing what she was doing, Griselda hurried through the tower (all that remained of Grunch Castle), down through the dungeon to the vaults where her dead ancestors stood in glass tanks, their flesh preserved in special fluid. The dead ancestors were in an unusual state of excitement, wailing softly, "Beware! Beware! Beware the powers of the night!" But trance-like, Griselda ignored them. She hurried down a corridor, dead ancestors on both sides, until at the end she came to a deep alcove where there had not been an alcove the day before. In the alcove stood a cabinet covered in chains, locks and snakes. As she approached, the chains and locks dropped to the ground and the snakes darted off in all directions. The doors of the cabinet sprang open to reveal a large book inscribed in blood, "How to summon the elements."

Book in hand Griselda hurried back through the vaults (where her dead ancestors were still wailing, "Beware! Beware!"), through the dungeon, with its instruments of torture, to the tower.

Griselda's guards, the Dim Daft Dwarves Julioso, Aliano and Benjio, were lying on the floor playing with the snakes and spiders. Above their heads floated Boris the Skull. Griselda kicked each dwarf hard and sent a thunderbolt which echoed in the bony head of Boris.

"Ow! Ow! Ow! Mistress, there was no need for that!" the dwarves and Boris cried together.

"No need! No need! Come here you lazy lumps of flesh and bone. I want you to go and get the ingredients for this spell from the village shop."

When the dwarves saw how many ingredients were needed, they groaned and groaned, and cried aloud, "But Mistress! Mistress! There are so many ingredients. We're tired out."

When Boris saw the quantities needed he was shocked. Although his evil reconditioning had failed twice, he was extremely brainy. Immediately he realised that the quantities were ten times greater than those approved by the Health and Safety Regulations issued by the Council of Evil.

"But Mistress! Mistress!" Boris cried. "The quantities are so great…"

14

Griselda did not give Boris the chance to finish the sentence. Raising her magic staff she sent a triple thunderbolt which whizzed around his skull, knocked him backwards, and bounced him from wall to wall. Then she kicked each dwarf three times (plus once for luck) and screamed at the top of her voice, "You lazy scum! Get out of here! Fetch the ingredients at once."

It took the skull and dwarves two days to fetch all the ingredients. They were exhausted. The village shop ran out of diced frog, sliced toad and slime of maggot. They had to place a special order. As the ingredients piled higher and higher in the ruined tower, Boris thought even Griselda must realise that there was too much, that they were in great danger, that there was no telling what might happen if all those ingredients were placed inside the magic cauldron.

But Griselda was possessed. Whenever Boris tried to point out the danger she simply sent another thunderbolt and kicked him out of the tower. It was getting dark on the second day when Griselda ordered the dwarves to tip the ingredients into the magic cauldron. It was strange the way no matter how much was tipped into the cauldron it never filled up, but when the cauldron began to moan and groan, sway and spit (as though it had the most terrible belly ache from over-eating) the dwarves and Boris shook with fear.

Boris cried, "Too much! Too much!"

"Shut up, Boris!" Griselda hissed, as she stirred the cauldron and chanted the spell to get the elements to rise up and suck the boys out of The Old Vicarage so she could eat them for her supper. She did not notice that every time she said the names of the boys there came from deep within the cauldron the fierce whisper, "And Boris!"

Until all was complete. There was a moment of calm. Then suddenly the cauldron began to shake and hum, and from its depths emerged terrible figures, a raging storm of malevolent power. The figures danced around the inside of the tower armed with clubs, slapping the faces of the dwarves, skull and witch and pinning them against the stone walls where they cowered in terror. More and more figures soared out of the cauldron, each more angry and terrible than the last. Ice, snow, wind and rain raged from their clubs as they roared and roared, and thundered round and round, crushing dwarves, skull and Griselda harder and harder against the walls.

"Boris, save me!" moaned Griselda, realising that as usual the skull had been right, that she had unleashed powers beyond her control. But at that moment the doors of the ruined tower, under pressure from the storm, burst open from the inside and the storm rampaged out down the hillside towards the village.

CHAPTER TWO

The boys' parents were sleeping soundly, as wave upon wave of raging figures (ice, snow, wind and rain) attacked The Old Vicarage. But as usual Snuggle the family cat was on guard and wide awake. He hurried to Julius's bedroom and got his brothers Alex and Ben to join them. With the help of the boys (who all had to keep very still and join their minds with that of the cat) Snuggle put a force field around The Old Vicarage to keep its inhabitants from harm. But as figures of ice, snow, wind and rain hammered on the force field outside the windows, and tried to get under the eaves and lift the roof, the cat swiftly realised that the powers he was fighting were far beyond those of Griselda. Unsure whether he could keep the family safe he urged the boys to join their young minds with his, to resist the powers of the night.

All would have been well if only the raging storm had not awoken the boys' father. With increasing alarm he went from room to room with a torch, shining it out of windows, seeing fallen trees all around the house, a tree propped up against the wall nearest the road, roof tiles swirling through the air and most strange and terrifying of all, raging figures of ice, snow, wind and rain hammering on the force field just outside the windows, demanding to be let in!

Then the boys' father did something stupid. He looked out of a window near the front door and saw a newly planted magnolia sapling swirling in the wind. "I must go outside and stake the sapling! I must save it from the storm!"

The moment that stupid thought passed through his head Snuggle, though upstairs in Julius's bedroom, knew what the boys' father was about to do. With a yelp the cat jumped off the bed and bounded out of the door. But he was too late. As he rushed downstairs the boys' father opened the front door and staggered out into the storm, round the house towards the sapling. The raging wind spun him round and round. A figure of ice bent low, knocked him down, and kicked him in the head. Crawling on hands and knees he pulled himself up and staked the sapling just as figures of ice, snow, wind and rain clubbed him to the ground, wrapped themselves around his arms and legs, then picked him up, and holding him upside down fed him to the storm. "Help! Help!" he screamed in terror as lightning flashed, thunder crashed, and the storm sucked him into its seething belly and carried him off towards the ruined tower.

The raging figures roared in triumph. "We've won! We've won!" they howled, for the boys' father had failed to close the front door behind him: the force field had been broken. There was a moment of stillness as the figures of ice, snow, wind and rain gathered and prepared to enter the house, to seize the boys and kill the cat.

Snuggle knew what was about to happen. With a loud meow he changed into a warrior, half man, half cat. He flung himself at the door. He tried to close it.

The door was almost shut when the whole force of the storm attacked, pounding on the door, determined to get in. The full force of the storm was almost too strong, even for Snuggle. The door groaned and creaked as Snuggle pushed on one side, the raging figures on the other: until with a mighty battle cry Snuggle slammed the door shut. But just before he did so a figure crept under the door and reared up behind him, snow swirling from his club.

From the top of the stairs the boys watched. The figure raced round and round the entrance hall, up and down the stairs, waving his club above his head, sending snow in all directions, covering wellington boots, umbrellas and works of art in a deep layer of snow. Snuggle leapt up with his cloak, tried to get the raging figure, but failed. Snow was falling hard. Snow began to mount the stairs. The boys should have been frightened, but were spellbound by the beauty. Until at last Snuggle leapt high, brought his cloak down around the figure and, with a twist, snuffed it out like a candle.

There was a gasp from the storm outside. The figures realised that they were up against a mighty power, a power even stronger than their own. With a great sigh the storm returned to the tower, and everything the raging figures had sucked up disappeared into the cauldron. First the boys' father disappeared, then Griselda, Boris and the Dim Daft Dwarves; lastly, a little girl the storm had sucked out of The Old Vicarage attic.

All travelled to Ramion. Boris, Griselda and the dwarves should have landed in the volcano of the Princess of the Night, but the capture of the boys' father was unintended. Something in the storm responded to his love of rock and roll. The spirit of rock and roll drew in the boys' father and with him it drew in Boris, Griselda, the Dim Daft Dwarves and the little girl (who was not at all happy).

The boys' father landed in a star's dressing-room, with flashing lights and luminous tiles, in the Land of the Dancing Furies. The land was subterranean, lit by two rather dim artificial suns, in the outer reaches of Ramion. (Not far from the Kingdom of the Frogs, it was fortunately largely free of the huge man-eating frogs which are such a nuisance in that kingdom.) The boys' father arrived in dressing gown, pyjamas and slippers, bruised and battered, glasses slipping down his nose, soaked through by the storm, shivering with cold. In the centre of the room was a jacket of many colours, striped trousers, lilac shirt with frilly front, and a pair of golden boots.

Hurriedly the boys' father slipped on the clothes and boots. As he did so, power surged through his body. "This is odd!" he muttered as, without thinking, he picked up a guitar lying on the ground (though he had only ever played air guitar and even at that had been pretty useless). The guitar felt good in his hands. He lightly ran his fingers across the strings and the dressing-room began to fill with music.

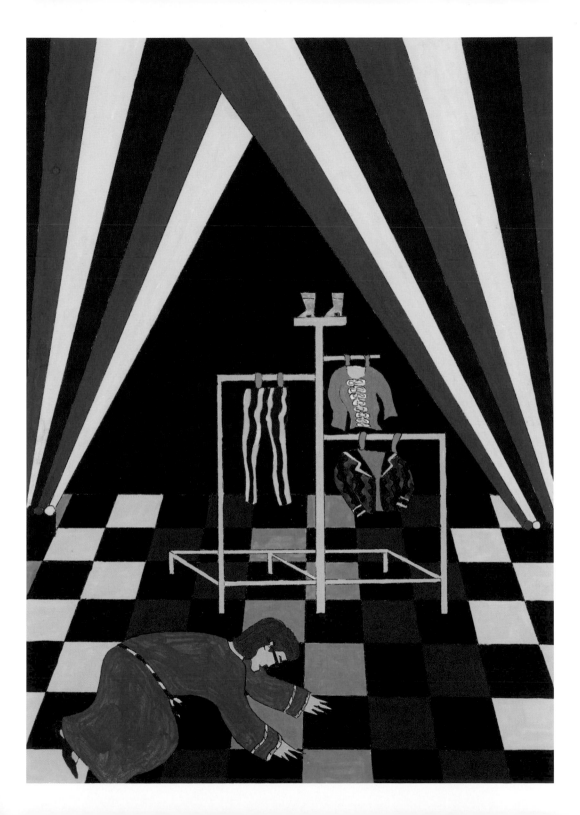

With a sudden (and totally unexpected) roar of "Let's rock, rock, rock!" the boys' father strode across the room and walked out onto a massive stage where the Dancing Furies and their band stood before a crowd of thousands of men, women and rock-crazed monsters.

At the sight of the boys' father in the golden boots the crowd went wild and began to chant, "Jimi! Jimi! Jimi!" The Dancing Furies cracked their scorpion whips in friendly greeting. The Dancing Furies (Allecto, Tisiphone and Megaera) were three sisters, clad in black leather with writhing snakes amidst their hair. In the past they had been Goddesses of Vengeance, travelling to earth to pursue the wicked, but those days were long gone: now they were only interested in dance and rock and roll.

The Dancing Furies hissed at the boys' father, "Sing, dance and play, or be consigned to a fiery hell!"

"A fiery hell!" he stammered in reply. "I'm feeling odd, not myself at all." Bending down he picked up a bottle of whisky, downed half the bottle in a single gulp, poured the rest over the guitar, and getting down on his knees set fire to it. The lawyer in him was shocked and cried in a panic, "I'm going mad! I've just set fire to someone else's property. Criminal damage. Punishable by imprisonment."

The spirit that possessed him retorted, "Shut up, you wimp!"

As the guitar burnt, the crowd went berserk, chanting in unison, "Jimi! Jimi! Jimi! Jimi has returned from the dead!"

The boys' father staggered to his feet. He began to sweat and tremble, to sway from side to side, for though the part of him possessed by the great rock god Jimi was (through long use) immune from the effects of alcohol, the part of him still normal found half a bottle of whisky in a single gulp a bit too much. Part of him was moaning softly, "Consigned to a fiery hell! I wish I had not been so stupid as to stake that sapling in the storm!" but the spirit of the great rock god Jimi hissed in reply, "Stop being such a wimp!"

Then the backing band launched into a pounding rock and roll beat and the Dancing Furies began to kick their thigh-length boots high into the air and crack their whips. A roadie thrust a new guitar into the hands of the boys' father. The rock spirit within him greeted the crowd, raising his arm like an emperor and shouting, "Hallo monsters! How is the Land of the Dancing Furies? How are you doing?" An aura of many colours shone around him. As the normal part of the boys' father moaned softly, "What is the matter with me?" the rock god (with the help of the golden boots) took possession of his body.

The boys' father danced wildly across the stage. He began to sing. Back home he always sang out of tune and was completely hopeless. Now he started low in a rasping growl, but when one of the Dancing Furies cracked her scorpion whip just in front of his nose he jumped an octave and started singing in a piercing scream. Then he grasped the guitar and (to his surprise) played a searing riff.

"Yes! Yes! Yes!" cried the crowd of men, women and monsters, going wild.

"Yes! Yes! Yes!" cried the Furies cracking their whips. "Now you're the front man of the band! Frankie and the Dancing Furies! We're going to play a thousand-year gig. You'll love it!"

"But I hate the name Frankie!" protested the boys' father, as the name of the band flashed in lights above the stage. "A thousand-year gig! I'll end up looking even more ancient than the Rolling Stones!" But the part of him possessed by the great rock god Jimi could not stop playing as monsters waved multiple arms and legs, popped swivel eyes, wagged darting tongues and jumped up and down in time to the beat. Even the men and women in the crowd went wild as the Dancing Furies kicked their thigh-length boots higher and higher into the air and cracked their scorpion whips.

CHAPTER THREE

T he Princess of the Night was in the anteroom beside Boris's body, waiting for the head. Impatiently she muttered to herself, "It should be here by now." After a long wait Albee the Albatross swooped in. She could tell by the glint of fear in the bird's eyes that something had gone wrong.

"Your regalness, your highness, your lordliness, your specialness, your evilness…" grovelled Albee.

"Out with it, bird!" hissed the Princess. "Tell me what has happened." When Albee explained that Boris's head had been led astray by the power of rock and roll the Princess was extremely angry. "I hate rock and roll! I hate all music! In the Land of the Dancing Furies they dance, play music and do little else. Disgusting! Repulsive! To think that the spirit of rock and roll could ruin my spell! I hate it!"

At this, the Princess got a little over-excited and returned to her original form of stinking gases. The stench was so great that Albee fainted. After the Princess had calmed down and assumed once more her mockery of human form she raised her magic staff and called upon the shadowy forms of the night to rise up out of the depths of the volcano and fly to her. Then she summoned her warriors, the mighty Gnargs.

The Gnargs mounted the shadowy forms of the night and flew out of the mouth of the volcano with the words of the Princess echoing in their ears: "Conquer the Land of the Dancing Furies. Abolish rock and roll. Stamp out dance and music. Bring me the head of Boris to go with the body."

Back in The Old Vicarage, Snuggle told the boys that thanks to a spell of the Princess of the Night going wrong their father had been taken to the Land of the Dancing Furies. They were not completely surprised.

"He is always dancing," said Julius.

"Really embarrassing!" added Benje.

"But this time he will have to dance for a thousand years. He will become a rock zombie," said Snuggle.

"We must save our Dad," responded the boys loyally.

"Your mother Susan as a little girl is also in the Land of the Dancing Furies. How? A strange cosmic freak. The storm blew her out of a childhood photo in the attic of The Old Vicarage. It carried her off."

"Poor Mum! - We must save her as well - Especially since if the Princess of the Night gets her as a child we will never be born."

"Good thinking, Julius," added his brothers.

"Join hands," commanded Snuggle, breathing on the boys, and they travelled through the void to the Land of the Dancing Furies. They arrived in the crowd just as the boys' father went wild on stage, thrashing his guitar, waving his hair (which was growing longer and longer by the minute) from side to side. The boys could scarcely bring themselves to look: it was so embarrassing.

"Mum would tell him to get a haircut," said Julius. His brothers agreed. At that moment the boys noticed Susan (their mother as a child) looking lost and unhappy amidst the monsters. They ran up to her and tried to cheer her up. "Hi, Mum! - Hi, Susan!"

Susan looked puzzled. "Who are you? Have we met before?"

"When you grow up you will have purple hair."

"I will not!" cried Susan in disbelief. "What would Mummy say?"

"Granny will not approve - But we like it - The colour of your hair was even mentioned in the last school play - And you'll marry the man on stage - He's our Dad."

"I will not!" screamed Susan in disbelief. "You're crazier than the monsters. Look at his hair. He needs a haircut!" In a panic she ran off.

"A haircut!" The boys laughed. "Mum's always saying that Dad needs a haircut! - She has not changed her views since the age of six! - Except about having purple hair."

Griselda, Boris and the Dim Daft Dwarves were also in the crowd. When Griselda arrived in the Land of the Dancing Furies she changed her soaking dress by magic. She was wearing a red 50s polka-dot dress suitable for dancing. Boris longed to have back his body, longed to be able to dance. Griselda was having fun making Boris jealous by dancing with the monsters.

"Oh Mistress! Mistress!" hissed Boris as Griselda spun a green six-armed monster by its arms and tossed it over her head. "Mistress! Mistress! Stop it! Stop it! Why not dance with me!"

"You don't have a body, stupid!" At this Boris floated off in a sulk.

Then Griselda saw Susan alone in the crowd of monsters. She had failed to eat the boys. "Perhaps a little girl will do instead." She went up to Susan and crooned in a deep husky voice, "Little girl, you look so sad. Are you missing your mummy? What is the matter?"

"I have had a really, really awful day. I had to dress up and have my photo taken. Then I was seized by a raging storm and carried here. Then I met some horrid boys who claim to be my sons and say that when I grow up I will have purple hair and marry that lunatic on stage - the one with the horrible hair who needs a haircut. It's not fair!" She stamped her foot.

"His hair is horrid, I do agree. But never mind, never mind," crooned Griselda softly. "Come with me. I will buy you an ice cream. An ice cream with fifty different flavours."

At the idea of an ice cream with fifty flavours Susan's eyes grew wide with delight. As she murmured "Thank you!" Griselda took her by the hand and led her away.

Snuggle spotted Susan hand in hand with a woman in a red polka-dot dress. "That's Griselda!" he shouted to the boys. "We must save your mother!"

But as Griselda and Susan disappeared into the crowd followed by the Dim Daft Dwarves, the Gnargs, mounted on the backs of the shadowy forms of the night, attacked. "Flee!" shouted Snuggle to the boys. "I shall hold back the Gnargs. If I am captured you must save your mother."

"And our Dad," cried the boys loyally as they turned and fled.

Snuggle turned into a warrior, half man, half cat. With sword and shield in hand he drove the Gnargs back. The fight was long and hard, but the Gnargs were many.

Wrapping flails of darkness around Snuggle's arms and legs, the Gnargs knocked him to the ground and dragged him off. They bound his arms and legs and placed a magic bag over his head to stop him changing shape, then threw him in a cage. In other cages were Susan, Griselda, and the Dim Daft Dwarves, but not Boris.

Later that day in the Sculpture Hall, Albee the Albatross landed on the head of a child frozen in the act of playing. As the Princess raised her magic staff the bird let out a terrible screech of fear.

"Still no Boris!" bellowed the Princess in anger as Albee bowed his head before her, trembling. "I want that skull. I want those three boys. I want them for my sculpture collection."

"But of course, your regalness, your evilness, your highness, your majesty …!" screeched Albee, bowing low.

"Shut up, you stupid bird. How many times do I have to explain titles? A King or Queen is called 'Your Majesty'. I am a Princess. You should call me 'Your Highness'. Nothing else. Now get me the skull and those boys. Use the girl, cat, witch and dwarves as bait, like goats staked to catch a tiger. I shall come myself to make sure that this time nothing goes wrong."

Chapter Four

From a place of safety the boys saw Snuggle dragged off. They gathered in a huddle, wondering what to do. "We must rescue Mum, Dad and Snuggle," said Julius.

"OK. But how?"

"Keep travelling. Never give up. That's what the Gardener always says. Something will turn up."

The Land of the Dancing Furies was full of different kinds of dance. The boys passed the entrance to a cavern where a man in a kilt was advertising a Scottish Barn Dance. "Roll up! Roll up! For one night only. Dance to the music of the massed bands of the Scary Scots!" Monsters hurried into the cavern anxious not to miss the dance.

"Wow!" cried the boys. "Five minutes of the sound of a Scary Scot and a boy or girl will explode!"

"Perhaps it doesn't work on monsters."

"I'm not waiting to find out."

But at that moment there was an explosion deep within the cavern and bits of monsters (multiple arms, legs and heads) and all their juicy innards came flying out of the entrance. "Yuck! Yuck! Yuck!"

There was a demonic ballet with devils in tutus spinning round and round ("Not for us"), a frenzied tribal dance with half-naked dancers, their skin every colour of the rainbow ("Again, no"), and blue she-devils dancing salsa ("Definitely not").

Then they saw a jazz club. "Let's go in there."

At the entrance to the jazz club sat a beautiful young woman with skin of shining gold, painting her nails a brilliant shade of pink. "Tickets, please," she murmured rising to her feet. The boys were about to say they did not have any when looking at their hands they noticed tickets between finger and thumb. "They will do nicely," said the young lady taking the tickets. "Follow me."

The jazz club was hot and stuffy. On the stage the band was going wild. The band was hot, so hot that suddenly its members self-ignited, burst into flame.

"Help! Help! Help!" cried the boys as flames shot all around them. "We're trapped," they screamed.

But as the young lady waved at them through the flames the floor opened and the boys found themselves in a water flume plunging down and down, round and round. The flume shot them out into a fountain in the middle of an electro dance club where robots were firing lasers above the heads of the crowd dancing wildly to the pounding beat. The dancing monsters were getting so over-excited that their heads shot off and bounced from floor to ceiling until pulled back into their bodies by elastic innards.

"Yuck! Yuck! Yuck! Let's get out of here."

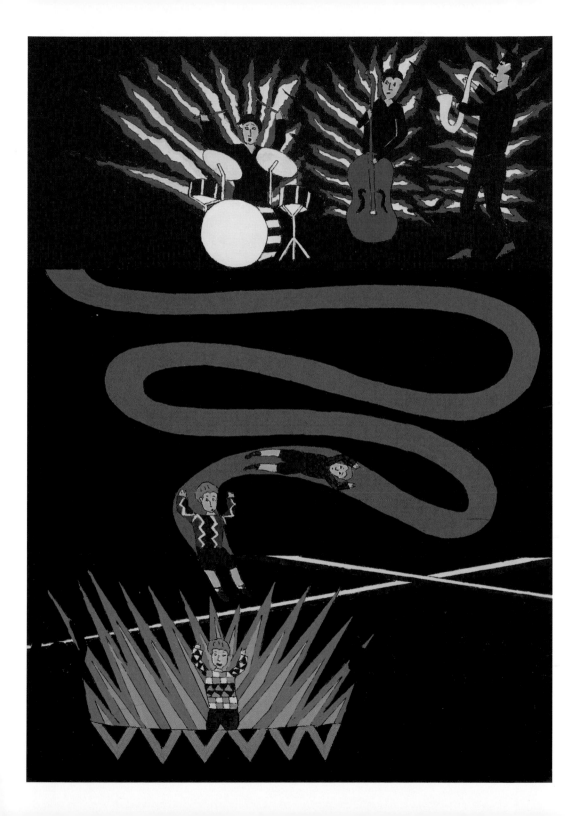

Fleeing from the dance club the boys found themselves in a cabaret hall where to their surprise they discovered their rabbit friend Scrooey-Looey who normally lived on a shelf in the nursery of The Old Vicarage. He was playing cards with Lucy Lucre, Brian Bread and Dolly Dollar, none of whom was looking happy, for Scrooey-Looey had won a lot of money.

"Scrooey-Looey! What are you doing here?" The rabbit yawned. "Gambling again! For money." The rabbit blinked. "Are you cheating? Mum and Dad would not approve!" The rabbit yawned and shuffled the cards. "We've lost Mum - And Snuggle - And Dad has turned into a loony singer with a band! - You must help us fight the Gnargs." The rabbit shivered. "Scrooey-Looey, you must help!"

"I would prefer to play cards."

"Scrooey-Looey!"

"Don't get so excited. I'll give you a clue. Your father is trapped inside those golden boots. If he does not escape he will become a rock zombie. But if he combines the power of the boots with his love for your mother he could do anything."

"Anything?"

"Almost. But you are keeping me from my cards." At that the rabbit turned away from the boys, shuffled the cards, and dealt.

The boys left the cabaret hall. Watching out for Gnargs, Scary Scots, devils wearing tutus, she-devils dancing salsa and all the other perils of the Land of the Dancing Furies, the boys hurried back to the stage. Their father was still playing. He was still singing like a man possessed.

CHAPTER FIVE

B enjamin went up to a bouncer with three heads, nine eyes and six-foot-long arms, and said firmly, "Our father is playing on stage. He's the one with the golden boots and the long hair. We need to tell him to think of Mum."

"Think of Mum! Think of Mum! How touching! How pathetic!" sneered the bouncer barring the way with his arms. "Get lost, kids! Don't think you can sneak round the other way. I've got my nine eyes on you!"

The boys slouched away and lay down gloomily in a corner, far from the stage. "What do we do now? - Come on, Julius - You're the eldest - We need an idea."

Julius thought carefully. "At rock festivals they fly banners. I saw one on television at a Dolly Parton concert. It read 'Joline is a tramp.'"

"Poor Joline! Was she homeless?" "Sleeping rough?"

"You're missing the point. We need a banner which reads 'Think of Mum'."

"Brilliant, Julius!" "Great idea!"

It took some time to find the right materials, but in the end they found a large piece of cloth, attached it to a long stick, and wrote on the banner in very large letters "Think of Mum." It was pretty scary edging through the mosh pit where monsters were jumping up and down, banging heads in time to the music. In front of the stage the boys raised the banner, waving their arms in the air, trying to attract their father's attention.

Although the music was fantastic, the spirits of the boys' father and the rock god Jimi (locked within a single body) were not getting along well. The spirit of Jimi reached for another bottle of whisky, but the boys' father dashed it to the ground, crying to the other part of himself, "You've had enough!" Then he saw the boys. "What are they doing here?" he murmured.

"Who cares!" replied the spirit of Jimi.

The boys' father then read the banner: "Think of Mum." Immediately he thought of the first time he met the boys' mother. A mutual friend invited them to dinner. After dinner she seized him by the hand and demonstrated a Scottish dancing swing. "I retaliated with an English swing and asked her out dancing," he muttered. The spirit of the great rock god Jimi groaned, thoroughly fed up.

The boys' father then remembered the holiday four months later in Ireland, climbing in the Macgillycuddy Reeks. At the end of the week they discovered to their surprise that they were engaged to be married. "The happiest week of my life," he sighed.

At this the spirit of the great rock god Jimi trembled, and with a sigh of "Love! Soul! Peace!" surrendered to the power of love. In a flash of blinding light the spirits of Jimi and the boys' father became as one, the boys' father completely himself and yet with all the powers of the rock god and the magic boots. He was free and, waving to the boys, he started to play a love song.

54

At the sound of the love song, men, women and monsters in the crowd joined hands, swayed from side to side and, thinking of girlfriends, boyfriends, their mothers and their pets, began to sob and weep. As love took hold of their minds and spirits all (apart from the Dancing Furies) became as one and suddenly there was a great explosion. One moment the crowd was in a subterranean kingdom lit by artificial suns. The next, in the middle of the song, the roof of the Land of the Dancing Furies (a great mountain top) lifted off, floated up into the air and with a roar blasted off into outer space. Light flooded in. Flowers began to grow, first in the ground, then in the hair of the men, women and monsters.

The Dancing Furies were not pleased to see the roof of their land blast off into outer space: they liked it dark and gloomy. When the writhing snakes on their heads turned into flowers, they screamed and screamed, beside themselves with fury. Becoming once more Goddesses of Vengeance they turned upon the boys' father. "It's all your fault, Frankie!" they cried as they lifted their scorpion whips.

The tails of the scorpions arched upwards, but as the Dancing Furies brought the whips down on the head of the boys' father the whips changed into bunches of flowers, and the scorpions into humming-birds of many colours. The humming-birds flew around the heads of the Dancing Furies as they rushed at the boys' father, fingernails outstretched. He merely smiled, blew the Dancing Furies a kiss (oh how they hated it) and propelled by the magic boots danced off the stage, guitar around his neck.

With arms outstretched Frankie flew through the air just above the crowd and taking Julius and Alex by the hand (Ben jumped up on his back), soared upwards across the side of the mountain where the roof of the Land of the Dancing Furies had been before it disappeared into outer space.

The Land of the Dancing Furies had been beneath a great mountain, surrounded by the Seas of Ramion. Now all that was left of the mountain was a circular rim (like the rim of a great volcano), bathed in sunshine, surrounded by sand and sea. There were other mountains in the distance. When the boys and their father burst into this bright expanse, they saw Susan in a cage with Snuggle in a cage beside her. Griselda and the Dim Daft Dwarves were in cages further up the beach. Gnargs were hiding with the Princess of the Night in groves of palm trees waiting to pounce.

The boys' father landed beside Susan's cage. He placed Julius and Alex on the sand while Ben jumped off his back. Smiling at Susan he sang a note, a note so high that it cracked the locks of the cages holding Susan and Snuggle. As the Gnargs, the Princess at the rear, ran towards them from the groves of palm trees he reached into Snuggle's cage, untied the ropes which bound him and pulled the magic bag off his head. Snuggle prepared to fight, but there was no need for the boys' father began to play the love song, Susan standing beside him shouting, "Yes! Yes! Yes!" How he was able to play the electric guitar with no apparent source of electricity was a mystery.

The guitar riff went right through the Gnargs. They had no idea what hit them. As the Gnargs staggered and lurched from side to side, Susan jumped and shouted and punched her little fists into the air.

The Gnargs began to dance in time to the music. With each note their arms and legs jerked up and down in a robotic dance like puppets controlled by strings. Then joining hands the Gnargs danced away as Susan shouted, "What a star! He's fantastic!"

"Come back! Come back!" screamed the Princess of the Night. Beside herself with fury she pointed her magic staff at the boys' father and bellowed, "I'll get you, Frankie! I'll have you for my living art collection!" Then she disappeared in a puff of smoke.

Susan clapped her hands and cried, "What a rock god! Boys I can't wait to grow up and marry your father. He's fantastic!"

"In his dreams," muttered Ben beneath his breath as the three brothers looked at their feet embarrassed: they wanted Susan to marry their father but when she discovered that he was a lawyer not a rock god she was going to be disappointed. There was just enough time for the boys' father to say, "Hi Susan! I'm going dancing! See you in 25 years!" before, at his command, the soles of his boots exploded, launching him high into the sky, across what had been the face of the mountain, back into the Land of the Dancing Furies.

As Snuggle prepared to magic Susan back to her home and the boys back to theirs, the boys asked Snuggle, "What about Dad? - He's gone back to the Land of the Dancing Furies. - The Dancing Furies do not like him. - He is bound to get into dreadful trouble."

"Don't worry about your father. I'll see he gets back home safely," Snuggle assured the boys. Then Snuggle raised his arms and gently breathed on the boys and Susan.

Susan called out, "See you, boys. What a rock star! I really don't mind marrying your father!" With that last cry Susan travelled back through space and time, enthusiastic about marrying the boys' father, even if he did have ghastly taste in clothes and shoes, and needed a haircut.

"A result! We can come into existence!" cried the boys, clapping their hands in glee as they whirled through space, back to The Old Vicarage.

After the Gnargs had danced away, Boris emerged cautiously from a beach hut at the other end of the beach. He floated to Griselda. He had her magic staff between his teeth.

"At last, you pathetic lump of bone. Get me out of here," Griselda cried.

"Mistress! Mistress! I wish you would treat me more kindly."

"Shut up, Boris. Just break the locks."

At this Boris, grumbling softly, sent laser beams from his eyes and burnt through the locks. Griselda and the Dim Daft Dwarves hurried out of the cages. Griselda was in a bad temper. She seized her magic staff. She was about to send a thunderbolt to echo in the head of Boris, just for the fun of it, when suddenly she stopped (the love song was playing in her head) and muttered softly, "Boris, you are a darling! Thank you for rescuing me!" and blew him a kiss. When Griselda realised what she had said and done she shook with disgust, growled, "I'm getting soppy! How absolutely ghastly!" and waving the magic staff above her head sent herself, the skull and dwarves back to the ruined tower.

Chapter Six

The boys' father came down in the Land of the Dancing Furies. Mid-flight he dropped the guitar, but he still had the golden boots and jacket of many colours. With the blasting of the mountain top into outer space the land had changed completely. No longer dark and gloomy it basked in strong sunlight and, like a desert after rain, blossomed. Flowers sprang up and turned their cheerful faces towards the sun. Forests soared upwards reaching for the sky.

The boys' father could not stop dancing. Time was different in that land. He danced for days and days. Elsewhere he would have been shunned as a lunatic, but in the Land of the Dancing Furies monsters, men, women and children streamed out of their houses and joined him in the dance, jumping high into the air, screaming, laughing, crying, until after about a week they returned home exhausted. By then, even with the golden boots, the boys' father felt tired, but still he could not stop dancing. He danced with every woman he met, took her by the hand, spun her round and round and kissed her on the lips. Soon he had lipstick on his lips, together with a rather silly grin. He forgot all about Susan and, as he did so, the boots lost their magic power.

As the boys' father danced between high rocks on the outskirts of a village, a tall woman suddenly stepped out and stood before him, swathed in a purple cloak, only her face showing. He held out his hand, to spin her round, to kiss her gently on the lips, but when she pulled back her cloak to reveal a scorpion whip and snakes in her hair he froze.

It was Allecto (which means Unceasing in Anger) one of the Dancing Furies. She and her sisters had not forgiven the boys' father for blasting the roof off their land and growing flowers in their hair. They wanted vengeance.

"Give me the golden boots!" screamed Allecto, raising her scorpion whip. He willed the boots to get him out of there, but nothing happened. The scorpion whip cracked just in front of his nose and shivering with fear he handed over the boots. With a sigh, the spirit of the rock god Jimi left him. "Now do the Fire Dance. Dance barefoot across the coals of fire!"

The boys' father had done the Sword Dance, the Circle Dance, even on one embarrassing occasion the Birdie Dance, but never the Fire Dance. He would have preferred to have given it a miss, but looking round he noticed that he was surrounded by streams of burning coal with no way to escape. He was in despair. He wished he had stayed at home.

"I must stop dancing with strange women," he muttered to himself when, to his surprise, he felt a little hand in his.

A little girl (barefooted like himself) was standing beside him. She stretched up on tiptoe and whispered in his ear, "Follow exactly what I do and you will come to no harm."

The little girl began to dance. The boys' father followed her every move. After they had danced for about an hour they fell into a trance and then the little girl took him by the hand and they skipped barefoot across the burning coals unharmed.

When Allecto saw that the boys' father had escaped the streams of fire she screamed in fury and disappeared.

The boys' father bowed low to the little girl (she curtseyed in return) and then continued on his way. By now he was tired and was dancing slowly. He was travelling through a forest when another tall woman suddenly stepped out from behind a tree and stood before him, swathed in robes of black, only her face showing.

"Oh no! Not again!" he cried, taking care not to hold out his hand.

The woman pulled back her cloak to reveal a whip of scorpions and snakes in her hair. It was Tisiphone, another of the Dancing Furies. Her name means Avenger of Murder, but from her expression it was clear that she regarded growing flowers in her hair as just as bad as murder.

"You are in time to join us in a dance of possession and summoning," Tisiphone cried. "I have summoned Kakilambe, the spirit of the forest. He will possess and consume your body."

68

The boys' father noted with alarm a huge shape passing through the trees towards him, a tree-shaped giant 25-foot high, spurting fire from mouth and nostrils. Kakilambe had been told that there was a stranger in the forest, a stranger who refused to acknowledge that he, Kakilambe was lord of the forest. That stranger must die.

The boys' father realised at once that he could not outrun Kakilambe. "I've had it!" he groaned. Then to his surprise he felt a little hand in his.

A little boy was standing beside him. The boy stretched up on tiptoe and whispered in his ear, "You must dance in homage to Kakilambe. Then present him with your jacket. Follow exactly what I do and you will come to no harm."

The boy began to dance in homage to Kakilambe, using his whole body to twist, spring and jump in honour of the spirit of the forest. Though the boys' father was tired out he followed every move, even when Kakilambe drew near and fear began to fill his body. Fire ceased to spurt out of the mouth and nostrils of Kakilambe.

As the boys' father danced, Kakilambe murmured to himself, "I was misinformed. By dance he acknowledges my lordship."

The boy whispered in the boys' father's ear, "Give him the jacket."

As the boys' father presented the jacket of many colours to Kakilambe, Kakilambe let out a sigh, smiled from ear to ear and cried, "Welcome to my forest."

When Tisiphone saw that the boys' father had escaped the spirit of the forest she screamed in fury and disappeared.

The boys' father bowed low to the little boy (the boy bowed in return), then passed on his way out of the forest.

By now the boys' father was exhausted. He ached from head to toe. He still kept dancing, but very slowly. He had not long left the forest when a tall stunning woman of great beauty suddenly stepped out in front of him. It was Megaera (which means Jealous). She was better at disguises than her sisters (changing her body to a shade of blue was a brilliant touch). Careful not to show her scorpion whip she hid the snakes in her hair with a brightly coloured scarf.

"Come dance the tarantella," Megaera cried.

The boys' father had never heard of the tarantella. Stupidly he agreed and stretched out his hand to Megaera. As their fingers touched a tarantula spider ran down her arm and bit him. Megaera laughed. It was some years since last she had acted as a Goddess of Vengeance, but she still enjoyed it. She let him fall to the ground. She laughed again.

The boys' father found it hard to breathe. His body began to convulse, slowly to turn black and die. "I've had it!" he groaned. Then to his surprise he felt little hands in his. Opening his eyes he saw the little girl holding one hand, the little boy the other, both urging him to get up and dance. "I can't, I can't," he cried.

"You can! You can!" the children chanted in unison, helping him to his feet. "Follow our moves. We will teach you the tarantella. The dance will expel the poison from your body. You will live!"

Slowly at first the boys' father began to dance, painfully copying the children's every move, then more swiftly as the dance expelled the poison from his body. "Thank you! Thank you!" he cried, bowing low, as Maki and Fey danced off hand in hand.

Megaera stamped her feet in fury, turned her back and strode away.

The boys' father had hardly recovered from the tarantella when the Princess of the Night appeared before him. By now one might have thought that he would have learnt his lesson and stopped dancing with strange women, but unable to resist a dance he raised his hand in friendly greeting. If the Princess had succeeded in taking him by the hand, he would have become part of her living art collection.

But at that moment Snuggle swooped down from the sky in the guise of a warrior prince, seized the Princess by the hand and with a single setting step whirled her off into outer space. The Princess travelled at such a speed that it took her over a week to get back.

Then Snuggle grasped the boys' father by the waist, with a gentle breath sent him to sleep and carried him back to The Old Vicarage. He left him in the drawing room, where next morning the boys' mother found him fast asleep. She could not wake him. He was still wearing the striped trousers, and lilac shirt with frilly front. His feet were filthy, covering the carpet with mud. Fortunately Snuggle had taken care to wipe the lipstick off his lips, but even so it was plain from Susan's expression that he was no rock god in her eyes. "Where did they come from?" she wondered, looking at the trousers and shirt with disgust. "And my goodness he does need a haircut!"

Later that day when at last the boys' father awoke, stiff and sore, he changed his clothes, then went outside. There were fallen trees all around the house. He found the boys climbing in the branches. A great cedar was leaning over the garage. Another tree was propped up against the front of the house. Part of the roof had been stripped of tiles. The magnolia was safely staked, but he remembered nothing of his adventure, not even staking the magnolia in the middle of the storm. The boys jumped down from the fallen trees and gave their Dad a hug. "What did you think of the storm?" they asked.

"I must have slept through it," he replied. "What a boring life I lead!" he murmured to himself. "Nothing exciting ever happens to me. Even when there is a mighty storm I sleep through it!" And yet where had the striped trousers and lilac shirt come from? He hurried back inside to hide them before Susan put them in the dustbin.

TALES of RAMION

Blown away by Frankie and the Dancing Furies?
More magic and madness awaits you...

Available Now:

THE DREAM THIEF

When the Dream Thief steals their mother's dream of being an artist the boys and their Dream Lord cat, Snuggle, set off to rescue her dream. The party, including their mother as a six-year-old child, passes through the Place of Nightmares (where butterflies with butterfly nets, game birds with shotguns and fish with fishing rods try to get them) and enter the Land of Dreams where with the help of Little Dream and the Hero Dreamhogs they seek the stronghold of the Dream Thief and brave the mighty Gnargs, warrior servants of the Princess of the Night.

ISBN: 9781909938076

CREATURES OF THE FOREST

In the magical forest there are Globerous Ghosts, Venomous Vampires, Scary Scots and Mystic Mummies, who (like other mummies) cannot stand boys who pick their noses. The boys are in constant danger of being turned into ghostly globs, piles of dust or being exploded by very loud bagpipe music. Thankfully, Ducky Rocky, Racing Racoons and the Hero Hedgehogs are there to help.

ISBN: 9781909938151

THE LAND OF LOST HAIR

The witch Griselda casts a spell to make the boys travel to her, but the slime of maggot is past its sell-by date and the boys and their parents only lose their hair. Snuggle (Dream Lord and superhero) takes the boys to the Land of Lost Hair, but Griselda follows, and sends giant combs, scissors and hair driers to get the boys. "Boy kebabs for tea!" cried Griselda jubilantly.

ISBN: 9781909938113

And these deluxe collections that include three or four Tales

RAMION
ISBN: 9781909938038

ROCK OF RAMION
ISBN: 9781909938045

SEAS OF RAMION
ISBN: 9781909938014

You can explore the magical world of Ramion by visiting the website

www.ramion-books.com

Share Ramion Moments on Facebook

TALES of RAMION
FACT AND FANTASY

Once upon a time not so long ago there lived in The Old Vicarage, Shoreham, Kent (a village south of London) three boys (Julius, Alexander and Benjamin) with their mother, father and Snuggle, the misnamed family cat who savaged dogs and had a weakness for the vicar's chickens. At birthdays there were magic shows with Scrooey-Looey, a glove puppet with great red mouth who was always rude.

The boys with Snuggle

Julius was a demanding child. Each night he wanted a different story. But he would help his father. "Dad tonight I want a story about the witch Griselda" (who had purple hair like his artist mother) "and the rabbit Scrooey-Looey and it starts like this…" His father then had to take over the story not knowing where it was going (save that the witch was not allowed to eat the children). Out of such stories grew the Tales of Ramion which were enacted with the boys' mother as Griselda and the boys' friends as Griselda's guards, the Dim Daft Dwarves (a role which came naturally to children).

SHOREHAM

Mill Lane

High Street

Church Street

The Old Vicarage

Elston Brook

River Darent

Polhill Arms